March 14
1989

To Joey,
I hope you have lots
of special times "up, down
and around your own
neighborhood!
Charlotte Towner Graeber

Up, Down, and Around the Rain Tree

By Charlotte Graeber
Illustrated by Jack Stockman

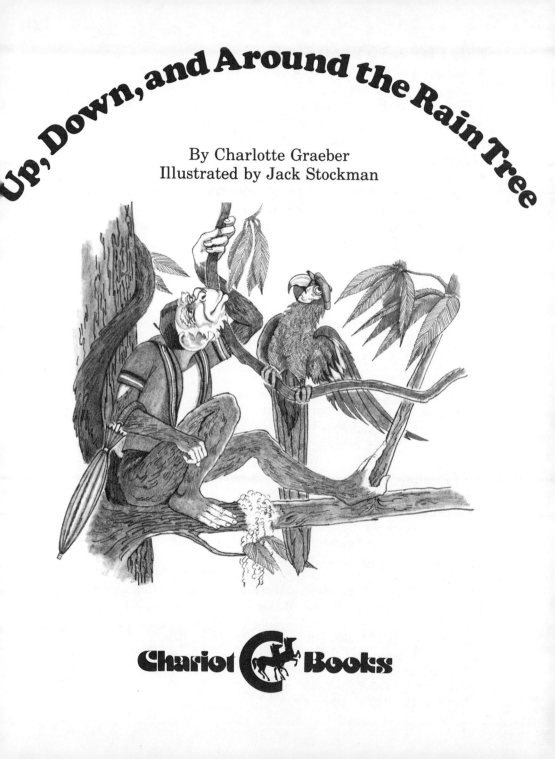

Chariot Books

THIS I LOVE TO READ BOOK . . .
- has been carefully written to be fun and interesting for the young reader.
- repeats words over and over again to help the child read easily and to build the child's vocabulary.
- uses the lyrical rhythm and simple style that appeals to children.
- is told in the easy vocabulary of the validated word lists for grades one, two, and three from the *Ginn Word Book for Teachers: A Basic Lexicon.*
- is written to a mid-second grade reading level on the Fry Readability Test.

Chariot Books is an imprint of David C. Cook Publishing Co.

David C. Cook Publishing Co., Elgin, Illinois 60120
David C. Cook Publishing Co., Weston, Ontario
UP, DOWN, AND AROUND THE RAIN TREE
Text © 1984 by Charlotte Graeber
Illustrations © 1984 by Jack Stockman

First Printing, 1984
Printed in the United States of America
89 88 87 86 85 84   5 4 3 2 1
Library of Congress Cataloging in Publication Data
Graeber, Charlotte Towner.
   Up, down, and around the rain tree.
   (I love to read)
   Summary: Parrot, Monkey, and other jungle animals experience the joys of treating each other nicely.
   [1. Conduct of life—Fiction. 2. Jungles—Fiction. 3. Animals—Fiction] I. Stockman, Jack, 1951-   ill.
II. Title. III. Series.
PZ7.G75153Up 1984   [E]   83-23155
ISBN 0-89191-786-1 (pbk.)
ISBN 0-89191-840-X (hc.)

CONTENTS

PARROT'S MANY TROUBLES

Parrot woke up.

It was dark in the Rain Forest.

Parrot put his nut sack over one wing

and went out.

The sweet nut tree was close by.

He flapped his wings hard.

He landed on a branch full of

sweet, round nuts.

"Ummm, sweet nuts," he said.

He pulled a nut off the branch.

He broke it open with his beak.

"Ummm, very tasty."

Parrot looked around.

Everyone was asleep.

"All for me," he said.

He began to pick the nuts.

He picked the biggest nuts first.

He picked the middle-sized nuts next.

He picked the small nuts last of all.

"Save some for me, Parrot!"

Monkey called.

Monkey jumped from the rain tree

into the sweet nut tree.

He carried a nut sack on his tail.

"You are too late," Parrot said.

"You got here too early," Monkey said.

Monkey picked the last small nut

and opened it with his sharp teeth.

"Mmmm. Best nut ever.

I must have some nuts."

"I have picked them all," Parrot replied.

"The nuts are mine."

Parrot dragged his nut sack back
into the rain tree.

Monkey followed through the branches.

"You cannot eat them all," he yelled.

"I will try," Parrot said.

He ducked into his hole.

Parrot emptied his sack.

He hid some nuts under his pillow.

He hid some nuts under the rug.

Then he lay down for a nap.

Picking nuts made him sleepy.

But Parrot could not sleep.

The nuts under his pillow were hard.

They felt bumpy.

Parrot got up.

The nuts under the rug were hard.

They felt lumpy.

Parrot had too many nuts.

9

"I will eat some," he said.

He began to eat the nuts

under his pillow.

Soon his tummy began to hurt.

"Oooooh. Aaaaaw," he moaned.

He covered his head with his wing.

Outside Monkey heard Parrot's cries.

He poked his head into Parrot's hole.

"What is wrong?" Monkey asked.

"I feel sick," Parrot cried.

"Too many nuts under my pillow.

"Too many nuts under my rug.

"Too many nuts in my stomach."

Monkey swung into Parrot's hole.

"I will fix warm milk for your tummy,"
he said.

"Thank you, Monkey," Parrot replied.

"You are kind."

Parrot drank the warm milk.

"Please take the nuts under
my pillow," he said.

"Too many nuts make too many troubles."

"Thank you, Parrot," Monkey said.

Monkey filled his nut sack.

He put one sweet nut into his mouth.

Then he swung out of Parrot's hole.

Parrot lay his head on his unbumpy pillow.

Now he did not have too many nuts.

Now he did not have too many troubles.

Parrot fell fast asleep.

"Give to the one who asks you."
Matthew 5: 42

PARROT'S GREEN JACKET

Parrot and Monkey were
going to a party.
Everyone in the Rain Forest was invited.
"How do I look?" Parrot asked.
He puffed his feathers.
He smoothed his bright green jacket.
"You look good," Monkey said.
"You look good in green."

"Maybe I look better in yellow,"
Parrot said.
He took off his green jacket.
He put on his yellow jacket.

15

"How do I look now?" Parrot asked.

"You look good," Monkey said.

"You look good in yellow."

"I can't choose," Parrot said.

"Green or yellow? Yellow or green?

"Which one will it be?"

"You are lucky to have two
beautiful jackets,"
Monkey said. "Wear
them both.
Everyone will
be impressed."

"You are right. I will wear
them both," Parrot said.
He put the green jacket
on top of the yellow one.

17

Parrot and Monkey left for the party.

They met Toucan going the other way.

"Are you going to the party?"

Parrot asked.

"Everyone is invited," Monkey added.

Toucan shook his head.

"I have nothing to wear," he said.

"Only this old coat."

Parrot looked at Toucan's coat.

There were holes in the front.

There were holes in the back.

There were holes in the sleeves.

"You are right.

"Your coat has too many holes to wear

to a party," Parrot said.

"I am wearing two new jackets."

Toucan looked at Parrot's green jacket.

There were no holes in the front.

There were no holes in the back.

There were no holes in the sleeves.

And a beautiful yellow jacket was

under the green one.

Toucan hid his beak in his feathers.

Everyone was at the party

when Parrot and Monkey arrived.

Everyone but Toucan.

Soon Parrot felt warm.

The yellow jacket felt too itchy.

The green jacket felt too heavy.

Parrot unbuttoned the green jacket.

He put it down on a tree stump.

21

There were no holes in the green jacket.

Parrot remembered Toucan's jacket.

It had holes in the front.

It had holes in the back.

It had holes in the sleeves.

Parrot left the party.

He found Toucan sitting on a log.

His beak was hidden in his feathers.

A tear was falling from his eye.

"I have two jackets," Parrot said.

"You may wear one to the party."

"I look good in green," Toucan said.

He took off his old coat.

He put on Parrot's green jacket.

Parrot and Toucan went back

to the party together.

Monkey was waiting for Parrot.

He had saved him some peanut cake.

"Toucan looks good in green,"

Monkey said.

"But you look best in yellow, Parrot."

"Thank you, Monkey," Parrot said.

"Yellow is my favorite color.

I think I will let Toucan

keep the green jacket."

"He who has two coats,
let him share
with him who has none."
Luke 3: 11

PUFFBIRD'S NEST

Oooooo! Oooooo! Ooooo!

The wind blew hard.

The rain was cold and wet.

Puffbird held her two Pufflings close.

"The storm will be over soon,"

she said.

She covered her Pufflings

with her wings.

Crack!

Puffbird looked out of her nest.

A tree branch was swinging

over her head.

Back and forth. Back and forth.

It was ready to fall.

"Run, Pufflings!" she cried. "Run!"
Puffbird and her Pufflings ran
out of the nest together.

Bang!

The branch crashed to the ground.

The tree branch lay across the nest.

It was crushed and broken.

"Oh, dear. What shall I do?"

Puffbird cried.

Parrot heard Puffbird crying.

"What is the matter?" he called.

Monkey heard Puffbird crying.

29

"What is the matter?" he asked.

"Our nest is broken," Puffbird said.

Parrot and Monkey looked at the nest.

"It is truly broken," Parrot said.

He tugged at the tree branch.

"Maybe we can fix it," Monkey said.

Puffbird shook her head.

"Our nest is unfixable."

All at once the Pufflings sneezed.

They sneezed four times in a row.
"Aaachoo! Aaachoo!
Aaachoo! Aaachoo!"
Puffbird covered them with her wings.
"My Pufflings are cold and wet,"
she said.
"What will I do?"

"I can help you build a new
nest," Monkey said.

"And Parrot can take the
Pufflings to his hole."
Parrot glared at Monkey.
Then the Pufflings sneezed again.
They sneezed four times in a row.
"*Aaachoo! Aaachoo! Aaachoo! Aaachoo!*"

"Very well," Parrot said.

"Follow me, Pufflings."

Parrot's hole was warm and dry.

The Pufflings stopped sneezing.

But now they jumped on Parrot's bed.

Up and down. Up and down.

"You will fall," Parrot cried.

He pulled them off the bed.

The Pufflings crawled under

Parrot's bed.

In and out. In and out.

"You will get dirty," Parrot cried.

He pulled them out.

The Pufflings opened Parrot's closet.

They hid inside.

"Stop! Come out!" Parrot cried.

Just then Puffbird arrived.

"Our nest is ready," she said.

The Pufflings popped out of the closet.

"Thank you for sharing your hole,"

Puffbird said.

"Thank you, Parrot," the Pufflings said.

"Thank you. Thank you. Thank you."

Puffbird took her Pufflings home

to their new nest.

Parrot smoothed his bedcovers.

He shut his closet door.

He was glad Puffbird's new

nest was finished.

He could see the Pufflings
safe and warm and quiet
under their mother's wings.

"Do not withhold good
from those who deserve it,
when it is in your power to act."
Proverbs 3:27

MONKEY'S BLUE UMBRELLA

"It's going to rain today,"
Monkey said.
"I can feel it in my fur."
He carried a blue umbrella
over one arm.
"We don't need your
umbrella," Parrot said.
"The sun is shining."
"Not for long," Monkey said.

It was shopping day.
When Monkey and Parrot
were almost to the market,

it started to rain.

Monkey opened his blue umbrella.

"I told you so," he said.

"So you did," Parrot replied.

Parrot ducked under the umbrella.

He did not like to get wet.

It made his feathers itch.

The umbrella was just big enough.

It covered Parrot's wings.

It kept Monkey's fur dry.

Just then someone came
splashing behind them.
"Oh, dear! Oh, dear! I am
getting wet!"
It was Sloth.

When she saw the blue umbrella,
she stopped.

"May I share your umbrella?" she asked.

Sloth was bigger than Parrot.

She was bigger than Monkey himself.

"There isn't much room," Monkey said.

"This is only a two place

umbrella," Parrot said.

It began to rain hard.

"I don't mind getting wet," Sloth said.

"But my poor hat will be ruined!"

Monkey looked at Sloth's hat.

It was red with a yellow flower.

And it *was* getting wet.

"Move over, Parrot," Monkey said.

"Make room for Sloth's hat."

Parrot moved over.

And Sloth ducked under the umbrella.

Now Monkey's tail was in the rain.

Now one of Parrot's wings

was in the rain.

Sloth's tail dragged in the
puddles behind.

Ahead someone was
getting wet all over.
It was Toucan.
"Rain! Rain! Rain!" he cried.
Then he saw the blue umbrella.
"May I share your umbrella?"
he asked.

"There isn't room," said Monkey.

"This is only a three place
umbrella," Sloth said.

"I don't mind getting wet," Toucan replied.

"But I can't stand water on my tail."

Monkey looked at Toucan's tail.

It was wide and black and
covered with feathers.

And it *was* getting wet.

"There is a little room in
front," Monkey said.

Toucan ducked under the umbrella.

"I am getting wet," Sloth said.

"But my hat is dry."

"My beak is dripping," Toucan said.

"But my tail is dry."

"My feathers are wet," Parrot said.

"And they are beginning to itch."

All at once the rain stopped.

Sloth stepped into the sunshine.

"Thank you for sharing your
umbrella," she said.

She patted her red hat as she walked away.

Toucan stretched in the sun.

"Thank you for sharing your
umbrella," he said.
Parrot shook the water out of his wings.
"I am partly wet.
But mostly dry," he said.
"Thank you for sharing your
umbrella, Monkey."

Monkey closed his
one place,
two place,
three place,
four place,
umbrella.
It was much bigger than he had
ever imagined.

"In everything, do to others
what you would have them
do to you."
Matthew 7:12

SWEET FIGGY CREAM PIE

"Sweet, sweet figs," Sloth said.
She jumped onto a fig vine.
The top was full of sweet figs.

"Be careful!" Monkey shouted.
Monkey watched Sloth climb
higher and higher.
Suddenly she slid back down.
She almost dropped her basket.
"Oh, dear. Oh, dear," she cried.
"I cannot reach the figs."

"You are too big," Monkey said.

54

"You are too heavy for the vines."
Sloth looked up at the sweet figs.
"What will I do?" she asked.
"I want the figs for baking."

"I am not too big," Monkey said.
"I will pick them for you."

Monkey climbed the fig vines.
He carried Sloth's basket
higher and higher.
He carried Sloth's basket
right to the top.

"Sweet, sweet figs," Sloth called.
"Pick them all."

Monkey began to fill the basket.

Toucan came by.

"Oh, Monkey," he called.

"Pick some figs for me."

Monkey picked five figs for Toucan.

Puffbird came by with her Pufflings.

"Oh, Monkey," she called.

"Pick some figs for me.

"Pick some figs for Pufflings."

Monkey picked three figs for Puffbird.

He picked two each for the Pufflings.

Then he filled Sloth's basket.

He filled it to the very tip top.

When all the figs were picked,
Monkey climbed down.
Parrot sat in the rain tree.
"Foolish Monkey," Parrot said.

"You picked all the figs.
And you gave them all away."

After lunch Puffbird came by.
She carried a jar in her wing.
"What's in your jar?" Parrot asked.
"Something good," Puffbird said.
She opened the jar.
She poured a cup of cool figgy juice.

"Ummm. Ummm," Parrot said.
"I love cool, cool figgy juice."

"The juice is for Monkey," Puffbird said.
"For picking sweet, sweet figs."

She closed the jar and left.

Soon Sloth came by.

She carried her basket on her arm.

"What's in your basket?"

Parrot asked.

"Something good," Sloth said.

She opened her basket.

She took out a figgy cream pie.

"Ummm. Ummm," Parrot said.

"I love figgy cream pie."

"The pie is for Monkey," Sloth said.

"For picking sweet, sweet figs."

She closed her basket and left.

Parrot licked his beak.

"Are you going to drink

all the figgy juice?
"Are you going to eat
all the figgy cream pie?"
he asked.

Monkey shook his head.
"You may have some," he said.
He cut the figgy cream pie.
Parrot took the biggest piece.
Monkey took the second biggest.
"I gave away all the figs,"
Monkey said.
"But I got some back again.
Awww! Cool, cool figgy juice.
"Awww! Sweet, sweet figgy
cream pie."

"Give, and it will be given to you.
A good measure,
pressed down,
shaken together
and running over."
Luke 6:38